CONTENTS

KIDNAPPED! ----------------------- 4

MASTER MUMMY MAKERS ---------- 8

MUMMIES UP CLOSE ------------- 14

EXPAND ----------- 18

FOOLING THE FOOLISH ------------ 26

MORE ABOUT MUMMIES AND ISABEL SOTO 28–29
GLOSSARY 30
FIND OUT MORE 31
INTERNET SITES 31
INDEX 32

We Egyptians believe people continue living after death. But to live forever, a person's spirit needs to rejoin the body.

Without a mummy, a person won't have a body to use in the afterlife.

Can you show me how mummies are made?

Creating a royal mummy is a complicated task. It can take up to 70 days to prepare a body correctly.

The embalmers, or mummy makers, are very careful. They don't want the body to rot. Here, let me show you.

First, the body is drained of all fluids. Then the brain is pulled out through the nose with a hook and thrown away.

Next, the body's organs are removed, except for the heart. The organs are dried out and placed in canopic jars.

Why do they throw away the brain, but not the heart?

Because the brain is worthless. We believe the heart is the centre of thought, and where the soul lives. It must stay in the body.

CANOPIC JARS

A mummy's stomach, liver, lungs, and intestines were each preserved in a canopic jar. The lids of the jars often were in the shape of Egyptian gods. Canopic jars were placed in the mummy's tomb near the body.

The body is then washed in wine and water. After that, it is covered in natron, which is a type of salt, for 40 days. The salt dries the body out.

The body is then rubbed with oils and resins to keep the skin soft. Then it's packed with cloth and sawdust to help keep its shape.

I thought Egyptian mummies were wrapped in cloth. Is that the next step?

That's correct. The body is wrapped from head to toe before it's buried. This scroll will show you how it's done.

11

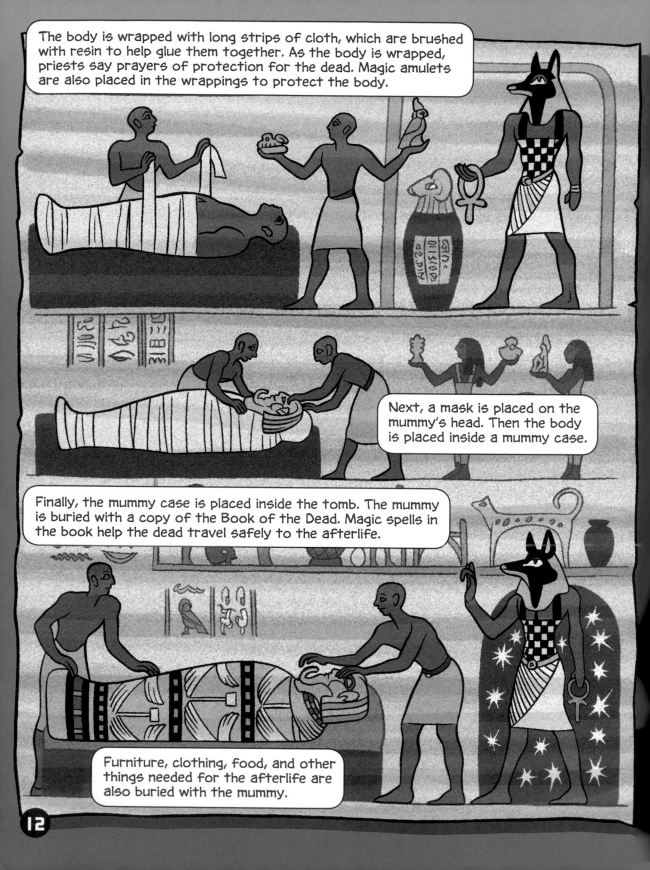

The body is wrapped with long strips of cloth, which are brushed with resin to help glue them together. As the body is wrapped, priests say prayers of protection for the dead. Magic amulets are also placed in the wrappings to protect the body.

Next, a mask is placed on the mummy's head. Then the body is placed inside a mummy case.

Finally, the mummy case is placed inside the tomb. The mummy is buried with a copy of the Book of the Dead. Magic spells in the book help the dead travel safely to the afterlife.

Furniture, clothing, food, and other things needed for the afterlife are also buried with the mummy.

THE SARCOPHAGUS

A mummy case was sometimes placed inside a heavy stone coffin called a sarcophagus. Only the wealthiest and most powerful people, such as pharaohs, were buried in a sarcophagus.

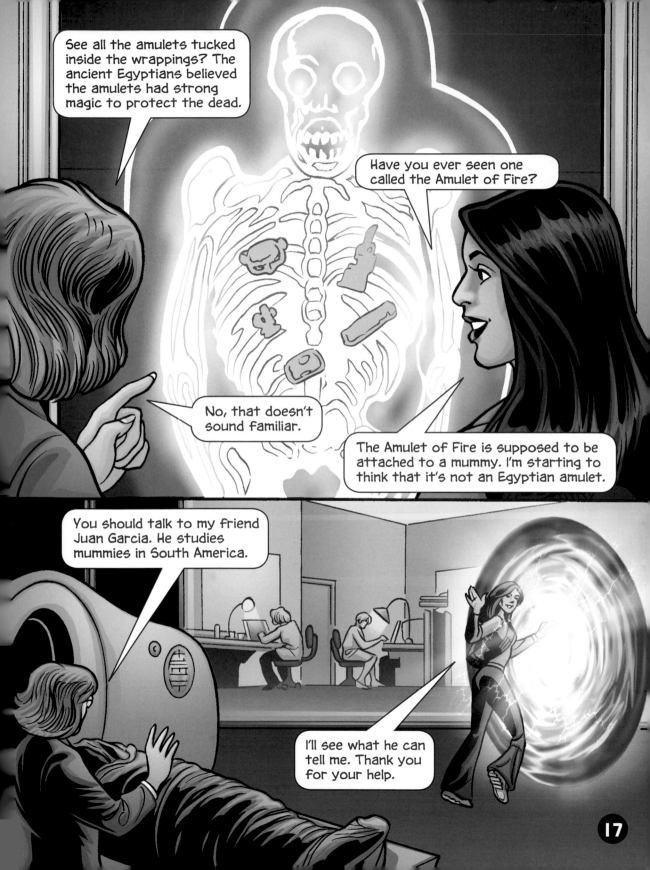

In Peru, bodies were preserved in "mummy bundles". The dead person's knees were drawn up to the chest. Then the body was wrapped in several layers of cloth. Over time, the body dried out to create a mummy.

Some mummies were made naturally. The Inca people offered human sacrifices to their gods high up in the mountains. The cold, dry climate froze the bodies and perfectly preserved them.

Have you ever seen a mummy wearing an Amulet of Fire?

No, but other natural mummies, like "Otzi the Iceman" or bog mummies, might hold some clues.

The Iceman was found in the Italian Alps. I'll go there first.

South Tyrol Museum of Archaeology, Bolzano, Italy, present day

The Iceman was discovered in 1991.

Two hikers found the well-preserved body frozen in the ice.

I need to talk to the scientists who studied the Iceman.

How old is the Iceman?

He's about 5,300 years old. Otzi is one of the world's oldest natural mummies.

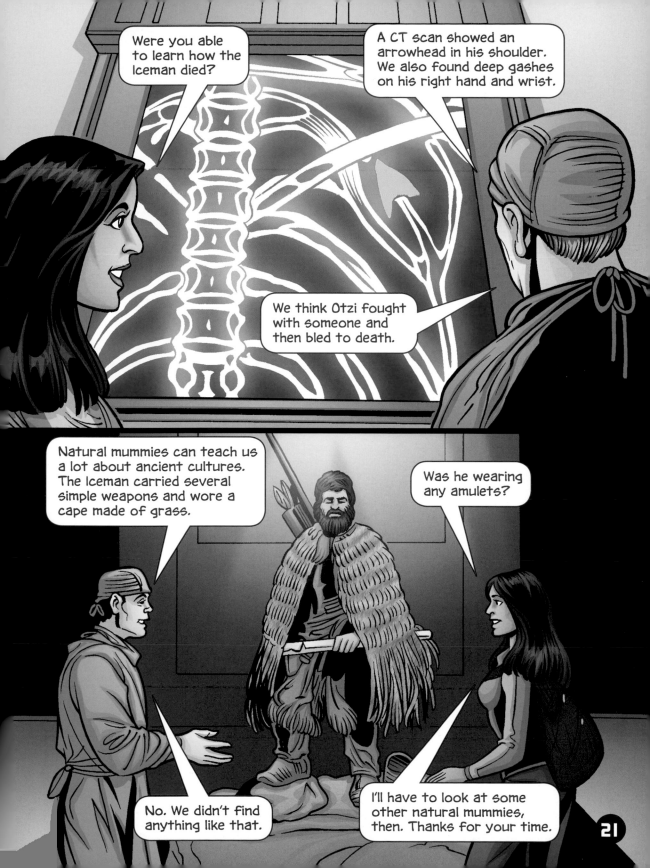

BOG MUMMIES

Peat bogs are formed from decaying plants in marshy areas. Over time, the dense mass of rotting vegetation becomes peat, which can be burned for fuel. Bog mummies turn a dark brown colour as they lie in the peat for centuries. Chemicals in the peat tan and preserve the skin so it looks and feels like leather.

The mummified bodies of eight Inuit people were discovered in Greenland in 1972. They died around 1475. The cold, dry air had freeze-dried their bodies.

British sailor John Torrington was buried in the Canadian Arctic in 1846. Scientists dug up his body in 1984 to examine it. The freezing temperatures had perfectly preserved his body.

Several mummies were found in China's Takla Makan Desert in the 1980s. The bodies are thousands of years old. The dry conditions in the desert turned them into natural mummies.

I'm looking at all sorts of mummies. But I still can't find any mention of an Amulet of Fire.

Near the Pyramids of Giza, Egypt, present day

MORE ABOUT MUMMIES

👁 Mummification was an expensive process in ancient Egypt. A wealthy person could be made into a mummy and have an elaborate tomb. People who couldn't afford mummification were buried in pits.

👁 Pharaohs aren't just buried in pyramids. About 3,600 years ago, the Egyptians began burying pharaohs in underground tombs in the Valley of the Kings. King Tut's tomb is located there. Archaeologists continue to explore the valley today.

👁 The ancient Egyptians also mummified cats, bulls, birds, and even crocodiles. Many Egyptian gods were linked to certain animals. The sacred animals were mummified and buried as gifts to the gods.

👁 Ancient mummies have not always been treated with respect. In the Middle Ages, Egyptian mummies were ground up into "mummy powder" and used as medicine. Mummies were sometimes used as fuel for fires too. Until the early 1900s, Egyptian mummies were often ground into a fine brown powder to make an artist's paint called "mummy brown".

👁 Many Chinchorro mummies had delicate clay masks placed on their faces. Several also wore wigs or clay helmets.

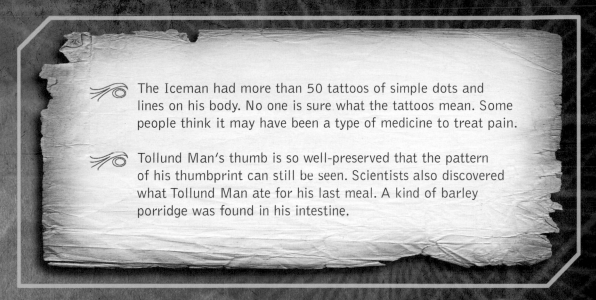

The Iceman had more than 50 tattoos of simple dots and lines on his body. No one is sure what the tattoos mean. Some people think it may have been a type of medicine to treat pain.

Tollund Man's thumb is so well-preserved that the pattern of his thumbprint can still be seen. Scientists also discovered what Tollund Man ate for his last meal. A kind of barley porridge was found in his intestine.

MORE ABOUT

Isabel Soto

NAME: Isabel "Izzy" Soto
INTERESTS: People and places
BUILD: Athletic   **HAIR:** Dark brown
EYES: Brown   **HEIGHT:** 1.70 m

WISP: The Worldwide Inter-dimensional Space/Time Portal developed by Max Axiom at Axiom Laboratory.

BACKSTORY: Isabel "Izzy" Soto caught the humanities bug as a little girl. Every night, her grandfather told her about his adventures exploring ancient ruins in South America. He believed people can learn a lot from other cultures and places.

Izzy's interest in cultures followed her through school and beyond. She studied history and geography. On one research trip, she discovered an ancient stone with mysterious energy. Izzy took the stone to Super Scientist Max Axiom, who determined that the stone's energy cuts across space and time. Harnessing the power of the stone, he built a device called the WISP. It opens windows to any place and any time. Although she must not use the WISP to change history, Izzy now explores events wherever and whenever they happen, solving a few mysteries along the way.

GLOSSARY

afterlife world where people lead a new life after they have died

amulet small charm believed to protect the wearer from harm

ancient Egypt the civilization that lasted for over three thousand years along the River Nile in Africa, from about 3500 BC

canopic jar jar in which the ancient Egyptians preserved the organs of a dead person

CT scanner special X-ray machine that takes hundreds of pictures to create a 3-D image of a person's body. CT scans can show soft tissues such as internal organs.

embalm preserve a dead body so it does not decay

organ part of the body that does a certain job

peat partly decayed plant matter found in bogs and swamps

pharaoh king of ancient Egypt

preserve treat something in a way so that it does not decay

ransom money or objects that are demanded before someone who is being held captive can be set free

resin a sticky substance that comes from the sap of some trees

sacrifice something given to the gods

scroll rolled-up document

tan use chemicals to turn skin into leather

temple building used for worship

tomb grave, room, or building where a dead body is kept

tomb raider person who steals objects from a tomb

X-ray photograph of the inside of a person's body

FIND OUT MORE

Books

Ancient Egypt (New Explore History series), Jane Shuter (Heinemann Library, 2006)

Ancient Egyptian Art, Susie Hodge (Heinemann Library, 2006)

The Ancient Egyptians (History Opens windows series), Jane Shuter (Heinemann Library, 2006)

Avoid Becoming an Incan Mummy, Colin Hynson (Book House, 2008)

My Best Book of Mummies, Philip Steele (Kingfisher, 2005)

Internet sites

http://www.britishmuseum.org/
Click on the "Explore" tab of the British Museum website and enter "mummies' in the Highlights Search field to see pictures and information about many different mummies.

http://www.bbc.co.uk/history/
Go to the Ancient History menu then click on "Inside Ancient History" and "Egyptians" to play the "Mummy Maker" game, where you prepare the body of Ramose, officer to the king, for burial.

 INDEX

amulets, 6, 7, 12, 13, 17, 19,
        21, 23, 24, 25, 26, 27
ancient cultures, 21
animal mummies, 28

bog mummies, 19, 22, 23
    Tollund Man, 22, 23, 29
Book of the Dead, 12
British Museum, 13, 14

canopic jars, 10
Capuchin mummies, 25
CT scans, 16, 21

Egyptian mummies, 8–13,
        14–15
    "Ginger", 14

human sacrifices, 19, 23

ice mummies
    Greenland mummies, 24
    "Otzi the Iceman", 19,
        20–21, 29

Lenin, Vladimir, 25
life after death, 9

magic spells, 12, 26
mummification processes,
        10–12, 18, 19, 24,
        25, 28

New Guinea mummies, 25

pharaohs, 13, 16, 28

sarcophagus, 13
Silkeborg Museum, 22
South American mummies,
        18
    Chinchorro mummies,
        18, 28
    Inca mummies, 19
    mummy bundles, 19

Takla Makan Desert, 24
tattoos, 29
temples, 4, 8
tomb raiders, 6, 26–27
tombs, 10, 12, 25, 28
Torrington, John, 24

Valley of the Kings, 28

X-rays, 15, 16